DISNEY'S MULAN

RUSSELL SCHROEDER

STORY ADAPTATION BY KATHLEEN W. ZOEHFELD

ILLUSTRATED WITH ACTUAL ARTWORK CREATED BY

Walt Disney Feature Animation

DURING THE PRODUCTION OF

Disney's Mulan

DISNEY PRESS

In appreciation to Howard Reeves at Disney Press who offered me the assignment, and to the entire *Mulan* crew whose talent, dedication, and generosity of spirit provided the inspiration.
—R. S.

Printed in the United States of America.

First Edition
1 3 5 7 9 10 8 6 4 2

This book is set in 12 point Hiroshige Book.
Book design by Edward Miller.

Library of Congress Catalog Card Number: 97-80163
ISBN 0-7868-3173-1 (trade)—ISBN 0-7868-5065-5 (lib. bdg.)

For more Disney Press fun, visit www.DisneyBooks.com

Adapted from
Walt Disney Pictures' MULAN
Music by MATTHEW WILDER Lyrics by DAVID ZIPPEL
Original score by JERRY GOLDSMITH
Produced by PAM COATS
Directed by BARRY COOK and TONY BANCROFT

Poem translated from the Chinese by Lei Fan.

"Honor to Us All" and "Reflection"
Music by Matthew Wilder
Lyrics by David Zippel
Copyright © 1998 Walt Disney Music Company
All rights reserved. Used by permission.

Additional illustration credits:
Page 1: Storyboard art by Dean DeBlois.
Page 6–7: Visual development art by Hans Bacher.
Page 17: Rough animation by Mark Henn. Cleanup of Fa Zhou by Frank Montagna.
Cleanup of Mulan by Rachel Bibb.
Page 72: Background painting by David Wang. Cleanup layout by Andy Harkness.
Storyboard art by Chris Sanders.

Contents

Introduction

5

Literary Inspiration

6

Artistic Inspiration

9

The Movie Story

17

Behind the Scenes

28

"Art is such a wonderful, spiritual thing; it's something we should always pursue. It's a gift from the Creator that satisfies something deep within us. Anyone who makes things with his hands and imagination, whether it's designing a car, a chair, or any of the countless things that we see and enjoy because someone thought to bring them into existence, shares that gift. The arts and creativity should always be encouraged. I'm grateful to my parents for having instilled and fostered that love in me."

Co-director for *Mulan*, Barry Cook

Introduction

Hundreds of pairs of eyes peer through a glass partition on an elevated walkway as daily visitors to *The Magic of Disney Animation* tour get to glimpse the activities that are a part of the everyday business at Walt Disney Feature Animation Florida. They pass by

virtually unnoticed by the Florida Disney animation employees. For the last three years all the energies of these talented men and women have been concentrated on creating *Mulan*, Disney's 36th animated feature, the first to be produced at Disney's Florida animation studio.

As with any animated film, *Mulan* began with a story idea. In this case the idea came from a centuries-old Chinese legend, a legend that has become one of the best-known and beloved stories from that vast, ancient country. The story of *Mulan* is most frequently represented by a poem accredited to the fifth or sixth centuries A.D. that is still taught in Chinese schools today.

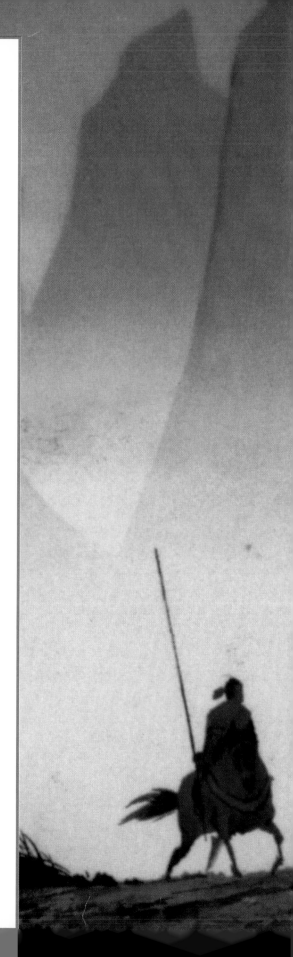

Literary Inspiration
The Legend of Mulan

Click click, and click click click,
By the doorway Mulan weaves.
When all at once the shuttles cease,
A sigh is heard with solemn grief.
"O my daughter who is on your mind?
O my daughter who is in your heart?"
"I have no one on my mind,
I have no one in my heart.
But last night I read the battle roll,
A roll consisting of twelve scrolls.
The Khan is drafting an army of awe,
My father's name on each beadroll.
Alas Father has no grown son,
Alas Mulan has no elder brother.
But I will buy a saddle and a horse,
And join the army in place of Father."

In the East Market she buys a steed,
From the West Market she buys a saddle.
In the North Market she buys a long whip,
From the South Market she buys a bridle.
At dawn she bids her family farewell,
At dusk she camps by the Yellow River.
She no longer hears her parents calling,
Upon her pillow the waters whisper.
At dawn she departs the Yellow River,
At dusk she arrives at Black Mountain.
She no longer hears her parents calling,
But Tartar horses wailing from Yen Mountain.
She gallops ten thousand miles,
For the war she has to honor.
She crosses lofty hills,
Like an eagle soaring over.
From northern gusts, through biting chills,
Echoes the watchman's clapper.

With wintry glow, of icy hue,
Light glimmers on her armor.
Generals die in a hundred battles,
Our warrior's back, how ten years fly.

Upon her return she is summoned to see the Emperor.
In the Hall of Light, she receives the highest honor.
She is awarded a promotion to top rank.
The Emperor bestows hundreds of thousands in prizes.
The Khan asks her what she desires.
"Mulan has no use for a Minister's post,
Mulan has no other extravagant want.
I wish to borrow a swift-footed mount,
To take me back to my home."

When Father and Mother hear she's coming,
They watch by the gate, bracing each other.
When Elder Sister hears she's coming,
She runs to her room, and dabs on rouge powder.
When Little Brother hears she's coming,
He whets his knife, flashing like a light,
And prepares pig and sheep for dinner.
"O let me push open the door to East Chamber,
O let me sit on my bed in West Recess.
So swiftly comes off the warrior's vesture,
And silently I put on my old-time dress.
Beside the window, I dress up my hair,
In front of a mirror, I rouge my face.
And when I walk out to meet my compeers,
They are perplexed and amazed."
"For twelve years, we fought as comrades-in-arms,
The Mulan we knew was not a lady of charm!"

They say to choose a hare, you pick them up by the ears,
There are telling signs to compare:
In air the male will kick and strike,
While females stare with bleary eyes.
But if both are set to the ground,
And left to bounce in a flee,
Who will be so wise as to observe,
That the hare is a he or she?

Artistic Inspiration

In the summer of 1994, several key members of Walt Disney Feature Animation's *Mulan* creative team flew to China to begin research for the film. They spent three weeks traveling thousands of miles through the impressive Chinese countryside and cities.

Visitors from around the world still marvel at the engineering feat involved in creating the Great Wall of China, which is almost 4,000 miles long. It serves as a dramatic backdrop for the film's opening sequence.

Dragons are a common design element in Chinese art, that inspired the creators of *Mulan*. This is a close-up detail of one from a wall known as: the Nine Dragon's Screen.

This lionlike guardian statue was often placed at doorways. In *Mulan*, the statues can be seen at either side of the gate leading into Mulan's courtyard (see page 19) and at the entrance to her family temple. When Shang and his men try to break down the palace doors to save the Emperor, they upend a giant statue like this to use as a battering ram.

This imposing entrance at the Jiayu Fort helped inspire the visual development piece (see page 36) for the Chinese army's triumphant entrance into the Imperial City.

The native trees and flora of China influenced the production design, helping to establish the setting.

They stood on the Great Wall, the ancient barrier that isolated China from the rest of the world for so many generations; they crossed rivers; they hopped on bicycles (the primary transportation vehicle for many Chinese citizens) and joined the early morning rush of traffic; and they visited many locations where it was claimed Mulan had lived.

Many structures in China seem to exist as a comfortable part of their natural settings, a characteristic that was applied to the design of the dwellings at Mulan's home.

The Disney visitors were immediately attracted to the pleasing architectural detail of the moongate. One was placed in Mulan's garden and serves as an important design element in several key scenes. (See page 53)

The highly decorative ancestral bei, which serves to honor and keep alive the memory of one's forebears, became a focal point for action in Mulan's family temple, as well as a means of revealing the personality and reverence of some of the film's central characters. (See page 52)

This trip gave the Disney visitors an opportunity to see and experience firsthand the variety and uniqueness of the Chinese landscape and architecture. It impressed upon them the incredible history of Chinese civilization. And it afforded them an understanding and appreciation of the Chinese people and the love they have for Mulan and her story.

When Europeans first saw the rolling mountain shapes in Chinese paintings, many of them thought it might be an artist's stylized, imaginative interpretation of hills. As any visitor to China can testify, these graceful and unique shapes are a very real part of the landscape, and the *Mulan* designers used them as frequent backdrops to the story's action. (See page 37.)

Observing unique architectual details helped the filmmakers clearly define the movie's setting.

Research into historical costuming, such as this dress from the Tang Dynasty, contributed an authentic look to the *Mulan* characters.

The Movie Story

Long ago in China, an important day in a girl's life was the day she presented herself to the matchmaker, who would arrange her marriage. This was Mulan's big day—the day she was to bring honor to her family. And she had bungled it, completely!

She led her horse, Khan, solemnly home. As he drank from his trough, she studied her reflection in the water. "The matchmaker's right," she sighed. "I'll never bring honor to my family. The other girls were quiet and demure—poised and polite. But me? I spoke without permission; spilled the tea! Even the cricket Grandmother Fa gave me couldn't bring enough luck."

She slumped under the blossoming trees in the garden. From the doorway of the house, her father, Fa Zhou, watched her sadly.

"What beautiful blossoms we have this year," he said, sitting down beside her. Then he pointed to a pink and white bud. "Look. This one's late. But I'll bet when it blooms, it will be the most beautiful of all."

He took Mulan's hair comb from her hands and set it lovingly in her hair.

Mulan smiled, the sadness disappearing from her eyes.

In the distance, they heard the village drummer announcing important visitors.

Fa Zhou steadied himself on his cane and made his way to the street. Mulan's mother, Fa Li, hurried to stand beside him.

The Emperor's Aide, Chi Fu, cried out: "Citizens! I bring a proclamation from the Emperor! The Huns have invaded China! One man from every family must serve in the Imperial Army."

Oh, no! thought Mulan. Father is the only man in the Fa family. But his leg is injured. He can barely walk, let alone do battle.

When the Fa name was called, Fa Zhou handed his cane to his wife and proudly took his conscription notice from the Emperor's Aide.

"No!" pleaded Mulan. "Please, sir—my father has already fought bravely for the Emperor—"

"Silence!" cried Chi Fu, angry that a woman had spoken in the presence of men.

"Mulan," whispered Fa Zhou. "You dishonor me."

That evening, Mulan watched her father as he went to his armor cabinet. He lifted his sword gracefully—swung it high above his head and lunged forward. "Aagh!" he cried. Pain shot through his leg, and he crumpled to the floor.

Mulan rushed outside to the garden, fighting back her tears. She sat at the base of the

Great Stone Dragon. A cold rain pelted the Dragon's stony face. "I won't just sit by and let Father go to his death," she cried.

Inside the family temple, she lit a stick of incense and placed it in the little dragon incense burner. "Please help me save Father's life," she prayed.

She crept into the room where her parents were sleeping, took the conscription notice, and set her comb in its place. Then, she took his sword from the cabinet and cut her long black hair. She donned her father's armor, mounted Khan, and together they thundered through the gate.

Awakening with a start, Grandmother Fa sat bolt upright in bed.

"Mulan is gone!!" she cried.

Fa Zhou awoke, bewildered. He noticed the hair comb on his table. He stumbled to his closet—his armor was missing!

"Mulan!" he shouted, as he threw open the front door.

"Go after her!" cried Fa Li. "She could be killed!"

"If I reveal her, she will be!" gasped Fa Zhou.

"Ancestors, hear our prayer," whispered Grandmother Fa. "Watch over Mulan."

At her words, the sacred writing on the temple's central stone tablet began to glow. Over the tablet, the spirit of the First Ancestor took shape and cried, "Mushu, awaken!"

The dragon incense burner's metal body trembled. "I live!" he roared. "So, tell me! What mortal needs my protection?"

"Mushu!" thundered the First Ancestor. "Awaken the Ancestors!"

Mushu sighed and clanged his gong.

The temple soon filled with the chatter of ancestral spirits.

"We must send a guardian to bring Mulan back," said one.

"Yes!" they all agreed. "Send the most powerful of all!"

"Okay, okay," said Mushu, "I'll go."

The Ancestors roared with laughter. "After all the trouble you caused last time!? You'll never be a guardian again!"

"Go. Awaken the Great Stone Dragon!" ordered the First Ancestor. He threw Mushu out the door.

"Rocky! Wake up!" cried Mushu. He banged his gong.

Nothing. He hit the statue with his gong, and the old stone crumbled. Mushu groaned. "They're gonna kill me!"

"Great Stone Dragon, have you awakened?" called the First Ancestor.

Mushu emerged from the rubble holding the Dragon's head before him. "I, ah...yes. I am the Great Stone Dragon!"

"Go!" said the First Ancestor. "The fate of the Fa family rests in your claws."

"That's just great," sighed Mushu. "I'm doomed!"

Grandmother Fa's cricket tugged on Mushu's tail and chirped encouragingly.

Mushu thought for a moment. "I've got it!" he cried. "I'll make Mulan a hero! Then the Ancestors will have to give me my job back. Mushu and Cri-Kee set out to find Mulan.

By early morning, Mulan had reached a hilltop overlooking the Imperial Army camp. "I'd better get some practice," she told Khan.

She took a manly stance and drew her sword. It snagged on its scabbard and clattered to the ground. "It's going to take a miracle to get me into the army," she sighed.

Suddenly, a great shadow towered on the rocks nearby. "Did I hear someone ask for a miracle!?" it roared.

"Who are you?" gasped Mulan in awe.

"Who am I?" cried Mushu. "I have been sent by your ancestors to guide you." He stepped out from behind the rock that had hidden him.

"My Ancestors sent a lizard to help me?" she asked.

"Dragon," corrected Mushu. He hid inside Mulan's kerchief. "Let's get this show on the road!" he cried.

Mulan walked awkwardly through the crowded army camp. "Try to act like them," coached Mushu.

Mulan strode up to a group of three soldiers and stared.

"What are you looking at?" asked Yao.

"Punch him," Mushu whispered to Mulan. "It's how men say hello."

Mulan hit Yao on the shoulder.

"Grrrr," growled Yao.

"Relax and chant with me," said Yao's friend, Chien-Po.

"Right," said Yao, turning away. "You ain't worth my time, chicken boy!"

"Say that to my face, ya limp noodle!" cried Mushu from inside Mulan's kerchief. Mulan cringed.

Yao turned and swung a punch. Mulan ducked, and, blam! Yao's fist landed on his friend Ling's jaw instead.

General Li and his son, Captain Shang, and the Emperor's Aide, Chi Fu, stepped out of the command tent and saw the chaos.

"When you have trained these recruits, you will join us, Captain," said the general. Then he mustered his own well-polished troops and rode off to the Tung-Shao Pass to stop the Huns.

The next morning, Captain Shang began training the new recruits. He shot an arrow into the top of a tall pole. "Yao. Retrieve the arrow," he commanded. "But wait! You seem to be missing something." He opened a box, took out two bronze discs, and tied them to Yao's wrists. "The first one represents discipline," he said, "the second, strength."

Yao inched his way up the pole. Then, CRASH! He fell to the ground, defeated. One after another, the soldiers tried to reach the arrow and failed.

"We've got a long way to go," said Shang.

One evening, after several grueling days of training, Mulan returned to camp. Shang met her and told her to go home. He had decided she would never be a soldier.

Discouraged, she turned to look at the arrow once more and paused. She tied the two bronze discs together and used them to shinny up the pole.

"Hooray!" shouted the soliders as she triumphantly reached the top of the pole and the arrow.

Still, Chi Fu wasn't impressed. "Those boys aren't fit to be soldiers," he said to Shang. "When I send the general my report, your troops will never see battle."

Mushu was listening. "Oh, no," he groaned. "How am I going to make Mulan a hero if she doesn't fight!?"

He snuck inside Chi Fu's tent and made Cri-Kee forge an official letter. Then he

patched together a soldier puppet with some leftover armor, set it on a panda, and rode the panda up to Chi Fu. "Urgent letter from General Li," said the puppet.

"Who are you?" asked Chi Fu suspiciously.

"We're in a war, man!" cried the puppet. "There's no time for stu-
pid questions!" He handed Chi Fu the letter.

"Captain!" shouted Chi Fu. "We're needed at the front!!"

Shang gathered his troops, and they trudged up the snowy slopes toward the Tung-Shao Pass.

In the distance they spied a plume of black smoke. As they approached, they could see a village in ruins.

"I don't understand," said Shang. "My father should have been here."

Chi Fu pointed to the valley below. The Imperial forces lay defeated—all, including the general, dead.

"I'm sorry," whispered Mulan.

Shang roused his courage. "The Huns are moving quickly," he said. "We'll make better time to the Imperial City if we go through the pass. We're the only hope for the Emperor now. Move out!"

As they forged through the pass, an arrow thunked Shang's armor and knocked him off his horse. Suddenly, a hail of flaming arrows filled the air. The Huns were attacking!

"Get out of range!" shouted Shang. "Save the cannons!"

They retreated behind a line of rocks and began to fire the cannons at the Huns.

"Heeiiaahh!!!" came the bloodcurdling cry of the Hun leader, Shan-Yu, as he led the charge down the mountainside.

"Hold the last cannon for Shan-Yu!" cried Shang.

The soldiers drew their swords, ready for battle.

Mulan noticed the mountain crest reflected in her blade. She sheathed it and grabbed the last cannon.

"Come back!" cried Shang as he watched Mulan charge toward the Huns alone.

Mulan planted the cannon and aimed. She yanked on Mushu's tail. Whoosh—a little flame leapt out of his mouth and lighted the fuse.

KABOOM! The rocket zoomed over Shan-Yu's head.

"You missed him," nagged Mushu. "How could you miss him??"

WHAM! The rocket slammed into the mountaintop and exploded, sending an avalanche of snow roaring down.

Shan-Yu lashed his sword at Mulan in fury. She jumped away and stumbled through the snow, trying to outrun the avalanche.

She was losing the race! But so was Shan-Yu.

"Auggghhh!!!" Mulan heard Shan-Yu and his Huns cry out as the avalanche buried them.

In the nick of time, Khan raced to Mulan's rescue, and she vaulted onto his back. Then they spotted Shang caught in waves of onrushing snow. Mulan lifted him out of the avalanche's grip, and Khan carried them both to safety.

When they had all reached higher ground, the troops gathered around Mulan and cheered.

"You are the craziest man I've ever met," said Shang. "And for that I owe you my life. From now on, you have my trust."

"Aaah," groaned Mulan. She touched her aching side. Her hand was covered in blood.

"He's injured!" cried Shang. "Get him to the medic's tent!"

After tending her wound, the medic stepped outside. Mulan's secret was revealed.

"A woman! Treacherous snake!" cried Chi Fu.

"I did it to save my father," she explained to Shang.

"High treason!" cried Chi Fu. "Captain? You know what must be done."

Shang threw Mulan's sword in the snow before her. "A life for a life," he said. "My

debt is repaid." Then, turning to the troops he cried, "Move out!"

Chi Fu sputtered in disbelief. "By law she must be put to death!"

But Shang had made his decision. He glared at Chi Fu. "I said, 'move out!'"

As the troops vanished into the snowy Pass, Mulan sighed. "I should never have left home."

"Hey," said Mushu. "You did it to save your father's life."

"Maybe I didn't go for my father," said Mulan. "Maybe what I really wanted was to prove I could do things right."

"The truth is, we're both frauds," said Mushu. "Your ancestors never sent me. You risked your life to help people you love. I risked your life to help myself."

"Well, let's go home," sighed Mulan.

An eerie howl stopped them in their tracks. They crept to the edge of a cliff and peered down. Shan-Yu had smashed out of his icy grave. Soon, his five strongest Huns were with him!

"They're heading for the Imperial City," gasped Mulan. "I have to do something"

She galloped through the city gates, with Mushu and Cri-Kee beside her.

When she found her comrades, she told them the Huns were in the city. "Why should I believe you?" said Shang. He turned away and climbed the great stairs toward the Emperor.

Mulan watched as the Emperor proclaimed victory. But, before he could finish, the Huns burst out of a paper dragon, knocked Shang to the ground, and carried the Emperor up to the tower.

Shang rallied his men and tried to batter down the palace door.

"Hey, guys, I have an idea," Mulan called. "Come with me." Shang stared at her stubbornly. Yao, Ling, and Chien-Po took off after Mulan.

She led them to a quiet spot, where she disguised them as women. Then, following Mulan's lead, each one removed his sash and wrapped it around one of the palace pillars.

Shang saw what they were doing. He took off his cape and joined them as they shinnied up.

Inside, they found the Huns guarding a door.

Mulan and her "girls" took the guards by surprise and overpowered them.

With the guards out cold, Shang burst though the door. He saw Shan-Yu's sword poised over the Emperor's head.

Shang charged toward Shan-Yu and fought him off, while Mulan helped Ling, Yao, and Chien-Po get the Emperor to safety along a zip-line of banners.

Then one of Shan-Yu's punches knocked Shang unconscious.

Mulan dove for his sword and cut the zip-line so Shan-Yu could not follow the Emperor.

"Nooo!" cried Shan-Yu. He turned to Mulan in fury.

Mulan grabbed Mushu and fled.

"What's the plan?" asked Mushu.

Mulan pointed to the fireworks tower.

"I'm way ahead of you," Mushu replied. He and Cri-Kee hopped on a kite and flew to the tower.

By the time Mushu returned with a rocket strapped to his back, Mulan had led Shan-Yu to the roof. The huge Hun lunged for her, but she dodged his blow. As he teetered, off balance, she kicked his legs out from under him and pinned him to the roof with his own sword.

Seeing the opportunity, Mushu lighted a little stick and handed it to Cri-Kee. "Light me!" he cried, pointing to the fuse.

Wooosh! Mushu guided the rocket toward Shan-Yu. Mulan ducked.

"Aggghhh!" cried Shan-Yu as the rocket carried him off. KAABLAAAM! Shan-Yu and the rocket crashed into the fireworks tower.

Propelled by the blast, Mulan fell down the stairs and landed on Shang. Mushu and Cri-Kee crash-landed nearby.

"Where is that woman," puffed Chi Fu, emerging from the smoke and rubble of the palace.

"She's a hero!" cried Shang.

"She's worthless," muttered Chi Fu.

"That," said the Emperor, "is enough. Fa Mulan, you have saved us all. And for that, I honor you." He bowed to her.

Everyone began to bow and cheer.

The Emperor placed his pendant around Mulan's neck. "Take this," he said, "so your family will know what you have done for me." He handed her Shan-Yu's sword. "And

this, so the world will know what you have done for China."

When Mulan returned home, she knelt before her father and presented the Emperor's gifts of honor.

Fa Zhou took them solemnly and set them aside. "The greatest gift and honor is having you for a daughter. I have missed you so."

"I've missed you, too," she said.

"Isn't it wonderful," sighed Fa Li.

"Great," said Grandmother Fa, "she brings home a sword, but if you ask me, she should have brought home a ma—"

"Excuse me," called Shang from the gate. "Does Fa Mulan live here? Oh . . . Mulan. I have come to . . . uh . . . return your helmet. That is, er...your father's helmet," he stammered.

Mulan and her father exchanged a smile.

"Shang," she asked, "would you like to stay for dinner?"

In the temple, the First Ancestor leaned out the window, watching.

"Well," said Mushu, "c'mon . . . who did a good job? Who?"

"Oh, all right," muttered the First Ancestor. "You can be a guardian again."

"Yaaaahhhh!!!" cried Mushu. "Guess who's back on pedestal five!"

Cri-Kee banged the gong in glee, and the ancestors cheered.

Everyone celebrated a happy ending to Mulan's and Mushu's adventures.

Behind the Scenes

Whether it's an original tale or an existing one, like *Mulan*, transforming any story into a meaningful, unique, and entertaining animated film requires many years of exploration, inspiration, and plain hard work from a dedicated team of filmmakers that number into the several hundreds. Nothing describes them better than *team*. For without a thorough spirit of teamwork, no animated feature could be produced, and none would ever have the richness of texture that comes from so many creative spirits working together and inspiring each other as they combine and dedicate their talents to a common goal. This team of artists, writers, composers, and technicians used the skills of their crafts, the tools of their medium, and the inspiration of their souls, to bring the filmed version of the legend of Mulan alive through animation.

Many of the creative processes occur simultaneously during filmmaking, as the story and characters grow and develop and take on a life of their own. Keeping all those things happening at once becomes quite a juggling act. In the case of *Mulan*, the role of "juggler" (and so much more) was assigned to the directors and the producer—Barry Cook, Tony Bancroft, and Pam Coats, respectively. It was their job to keep the film's many components flowing in a continuous rhythm, always maintaining a careful eye and a steady hand, while at the same time avoiding disastrous collisions or letting something fall by the wayside. And it was through their diligence and spirit that the hundreds of hands and minds required to create *Mulan* were able to pull together to produce a story that has a unified vision and heart.

Barry Cook, Pam Coats, and Tony Bancroft pose with maquettes, sculptures that help the animators envision the *Mulan* characters dimensionally.

Helping the directors and producer throughout the entire filmmaking process were the many members of their support staff. They never drew a line; they never added a dab of color to a single frame of film. Yet, by organizing the film's many components and keeping them on track, they were the ones who kept the life flowing through the arteries that fed the production. Without their dedicated commitment, the production's pulse would have faltered, its heart stopped.

Lastly, as the film took shape over its five-year production period, *Mulan* received suggestions, proddings, and approval from Michael Eisner, Roy Disney, Peter Schneider, and Thomas Schumacher—a group of Disney executives whose commitment to continuing the heritage of Disney animation has been essential in reawakening, revitalizing, and advancing the art form known as the animated feature.

The Producer

Many key members of the *Mulan* production team had already been working for several months on the film when Pam Coats agreed to join them as producer. The spirit of family that evolves through the course of a production had already been established on a previous film between first-time feature producer Pam and first-time feature director Barry Cook. Barry greeted Pam with a hug and assured her, "I know we can do this together." This, of course, meant overseeing everything—the design of the characters and their costumes, the settings, the art direction, casting the actors who would bring the characters alive through their vocal characterizations, and every other aspect of animated filmmaking.

Pam describes the role of producer as primarily helping to balance all the pieces of the movie so that directors Barry Cook and Tony Bancroft can realize their vision for the film. "It's also my job," she adds with a laugh, "to see that the movie is delivered on time!" It wasn't long after joining the *Mulan* team that Pam fell in love with both the story and its central character, as well as the group of dedicated people with whom she would be working for the next five years.

Early on, Pam recognized that the film conveyed a very important message: to thine own self be true. By acting in accordance to that precept, the central character, Mulan, is able to succeed against the odds imposed by her society. Pam saw the character of Mulan develop into an individual whom she could personally feel for and care about. "Everyone contributed to help make Mulan a thinking, feeling human being, who acts out of love for other people. She's a completely unselfish hero."

Storyboard art by Dean DeBlois

In story meetings, Pam, frequently the only woman present, was impressed with how the men could get inside the character of Mulan and bring out what she was thinking and feeling. By treating Mulan as a "person" and focusing on her, they always managed to keep the story, which contains epic elements, on track and retain its human quality.

Mulan is revealed as a resourceful, determined, unselfish, and caring person as a result of the story team's treating her as an individual with her own unique strengths. Storyboard art by Chris Sanders, Dean DeBlois, and Chris Williams.

There were times, quite naturally, when Pam would have to push for some sequences to be handled with a certain sensitivity. The men became accustomed to hearing Pam say, "Trust me on this, it's a woman thing."

Yang

Yin

A prevalent design in China is the Yin and Yang symbol, the balance of positive and negative, of male and female, which can be seen on the pendant Mulan receives from her grandmother. Without consciously striving for that result, the story development team achieved its own Yin and Yang, with the creative contributions of the men, balanced by Pam's assessments and additions.

"I've also learned a lot from the story team," Pam acknowledges. "When the avalanche scene was being developed, I saw it as an action-packed 'guy thing.' What Chris Sanders and the others achieved in their storyboards, however, was action continuously interspersed with character—sometimes humorous, sometimes noble. Characters weren't just bodies being swept away by a force of nature; they continued to reveal and exhibit their personalities and spirit."

Pam found the trip to China, taken by some of the key artistic leaders, was an important experience in gaining visual inspiration for the film, as well as a feel for the people, the countryside, and the importance of the *Mulan* legend even to this day. "We did an enormous amount of research, much of which was able to find its way into the film—chess and gunpowder, both developed by the Chinese; crickets as good luck symbols; ancestral beis and the reverence shown to one's forebears; the fire signals atop the Great Wall. I'm pleased that the essence of our experiences in China has been incorporated into so much of the film."

Storyboard art by Dean DeBlois

The Directing Team

Because of the hundreds of personnel, and the complexities of making an animated film, Disney Feature Animation has found that it works best to establish directing teams, such as Barry Cook and Tony Bancroft. They shared the responsibility for making all the artistic decisions throughout the creative process, such as how best to introduce the initial conflict that motivates the story's events (in this case the breaching of the Great Wall of China by Shan-Yu and his invading troops); how a fanciful dragon statue, brought to life by Mulan's First Ancestor, sounds when he talks; or how quickly Mulan should walk across the room when she takes her father's conscription notice.

Rough animation by Tom Bancrott

The directors welcomed the team approach to meeting the challenges of filmmaking. "When we have had opposite views about how something should be handled," Tony commented, "our compromises have made the film better. We both had differing ideas about what color Mulan's dress should be at the end of the film. When we decided to use both colors on her outfit, we felt we had come up with something gorgeous."

Several design approaches and color schemes were explored for Mulan's Act III dress before everyone was satisfied with the result.

33

Mushu: Urgent news . . .

. . . from the general.

Mushu: Excuse me, the question is,
"Who are you?"

Mushu: I should have your hat for that.
Snatch it right off your head!

Responding to countless questions, both large and small, is a big part of the
directors' daily decision-making schedule. Decisions are reached, according to Barry,
"by getting all participants to agree and feel they've reached the best conclusion. And
when a group of people get excited about doing something, great things can happen. The
scene with Mushu and the puppet on the panda was thought to be too bizarre by some
of the crew, but the story artists, animators, and directors all believed in it. Their spirited,
creative approach to this scene has produced one of the film's funniest moments."

Chi Fu: Who are you?

Mushu: But I'm feeling gracious today
so carry on before I report you.

Storyboard art by John Sanford and Tim Hodge

Barry offered another important aspect of the director's role: "Finding the right person for the right job, and helping them to do it the best they can."

Tony found it exciting to find the ways to capture and maintain the visual style for the film put forward by production designer Hans Bacher and the marvelous character stylings of Chen-Yi Chang. "And the day-to-day work of the entire crew was so inspiring it motivated me also." Barry looked for "the universal truths that could be a part of the story, those things that are funny, meaningful, sad, and true, that people will recognize and enjoy." Both men received the satisfaction of meeting the challenges created by the production, and working with a talented team to make their vision a reality.

Visual Development

When the basic story outline for *Mulan* was established, a group of visual development artists began their work. Using the inspiration from the field trip to China, and immersing themselves in literary and art research from China's rich heritage, the visual development team explored the look of the settings, the style and costuming of the characters, and the drama and sweep of the story line. Some of the ideas from this stage of the film's development found their way into the final film; some were incorporated into the film for a while but then discarded when a better approach was discovered.

Alex Niño

Paul Felix

All of them served to help the entire crew understand the visual and story possibilities and to spark additional inspiration from the whole creative team.

Robert Stanton

Sai Ping Lok

Production Design

"Poetic simplicity." These two words describe the design philosophy and the look that infuses every aspect of the visual appearance of *Mulan*. The look is the result of a long period of study and exploration. Production designer Hans Bacher knew that *Mulan* would have to be entertaining for a broad Western audience who may not be familiar with Chinese art or culture. At the same time, he wanted to introduce a look for this film that would be all its own and would clearly define the film's subject—a story taking place in China about 400–500 A.D. Using elements of Chinese drawing and painting, Hans achieved his goal of creating a look for *Mulan* that reminds the viewer of Chinese art, but is also not too far removed from that viewer's understanding.

Visual development art by Hans Bacher

In order to establish China as the location for the movie's events, Hans chose to incorporate those natural elements from Chinese art that are typically Chinese, such as the unique mountain shapes and trees. Architecture, too, firmly helped identify the story's locale. An additional influence from Chinese art was that details were not allowed to intrude on the main point of interest in the scene. A soft, out of focus look was applied to many areas of the background, leaving detail for the primary story action. Empty space was added to backgrounds through the use of fog, mist, or even smoke, further giving the backgrounds open areas for the story's action.

This uncluttered look—clearly establishing a unique place and time period—provided *Mulan* with the poetic simplicity that marks every aspect of the production design.

Story Development

Just as with live-action moviemaking, a script is written for an animated feature. In animation, the next step is to create the storyboards—large moveable panels of pinned-up drawings and dialogue that look very much like oversized comic book pages—for each of the movie's sequences. This task falls to a team of artist-writers who flesh out the script; develop the characters, as well as the story line; and even take the first stabs at art direction and layout.

Head of story Chris Sanders said that although he began the process by pushing an unwilling and delicate story forward, eventually the story and characters developed such strong individuality that they began dictating their own directions and needs. Being responsive to those needs led him into creating what was right for the production.

Fa Zhou: My, my, what beautiful blossoms
we have this year.

Fa Zhou: But look . . . this one's late.
But I'll bet that when it blooms . . .

. . . it will be the most beautiful of all.

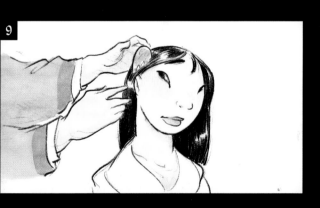

Story artists continually clarify the reasons for a character's actions and development. When Chris wanted to make audiences understand the love Mulan has for her
father, Fa Zhou—a love that compels her to defy tradition and put her own life at
risk—he devised one of the film's most eloquent and tender moments. In a lovely garden
setting, embraced by the delicate beauty of flowering trees, Mulan's dispirited mood is
gently lifted by her father's love, understanding, and faith in her.

Story artist Dean DeBlois sees the story artist's role as taking the broader issues of the script and making the film shine. His work on sequence six, in which Mulan makes the decision to take her father's place in the army, steals his conscription notice, disguises herself as a man in her father's armor, and rides off toward an uncertain future is, in itself, a perfect example of fulfilling that precept. The scene was handed to Dean as a

3

4

single sentence. In his hands it turned into just over two minutes of screen time without a single word of dialogue, driven by a compelling visual thrust, that shows Mulan move from meticulous, ceremonious action, to calculated, deliberate movement, and then finally to a fully unleashed, no-turning-back drive as she thunders off into the stormy darkness.

7

8

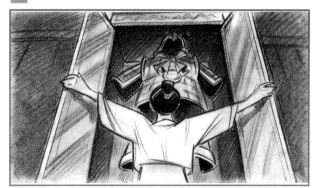

11

12

43

Character Design

Chen-Yi Chang was not a staff member of Walt Disney Feature Animation when work on *Mulan* first began. When he heard about the project, he recognized it as the chance of a lifetime. Having grown up in Taipei, Taiwan, Chen-Yi remembered the legend of Mulan as an important part of his childhood.

Chen-Yi brought more to the *Mulan* team than just an interest in the subject matter. He served the production as a resident scholar, who could direct his Western colleagues in Chinese architecture, history, costuming, and traditions. However, his main role, one that would span four years of creative output, was to design the hundreds of characters, both human and animal, who would come alive through animation.

"Some characters take a long time to develop. Khan is particularly satisfying to me because I had a strong vision of him right from the start," Chen-Yi explains.

Supervising animator Alex Kupershmidt concurs. "After we began trying to develop Khan's look for animation, we found we had come right back to Chen-Yi's original design. It was all there."

44

As with other members of the development team, Chen-Yi used ancient Chinese paintings, drawings, and sculptures for inspiration in designing the look of the characters. But to serve the visual language of animation, he chose to filter that traditional Chinese look through a modern point of view, utilize its bigger and simpler ideas, and establish a simplicity of line that relied heavily on the grace and rhythm of an S curve. He then worked with the animators to ensure a consistent look throughout the film. Reviewing the final animation, there is a noticeable lack of interior linework and distracting detail. It is both bold and poetic, giving the animation a graceful fluidity, the result of the close collaboration and respect between character designer Chen-Yi and the team of artists who brought the characters to life through their thousands of animation drawings.

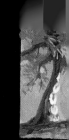

Art Direction

Working closely with the production designer and the directors, art director Ric Sluiter oversaw the film's visual elements. From layout design, to background painting, to the full range of colors for all of *Mulan's* characters, Ric made sure that all elements continued to be true to the overall production design and existed harmoniously and effectively from sequence to sequence. "A film's art direction is wrong if it is so strong it stands out on its own. It is there to help understand the story and the characters, not overpower them," Ric explained.

Color keys are small paintings that simply, but effectively, show the backgrounds and characters for the scenes in a sequence. Placed side by side, the color keys show how well the color captures the required mood and flows from scene to scene throughout the sequence.

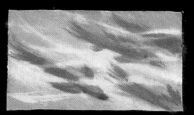

The color keys for the song sequence "I'll Make a Man Out of You" show how color creates the illusion of the passage of time over many days, as well as how color will convey Mulan's moods as she goes from discouraging failure (darker, subdued scenes) to success (increasingly brighter colors).

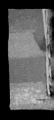

Seq. 9 i'll MaKe a MaN out of You.

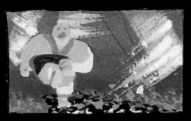

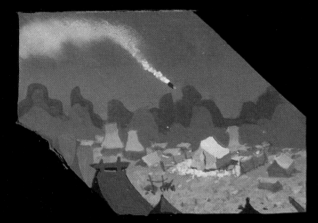

Color keys by Robert Stanton

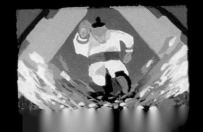

Visual development art for *Bambi* (1942) became one of *Mulan's* sources of inspiration.

Ric found inspiration from many sources. Hans Bacher's vision for the film was obviously important, as was studying the art from China's Tang Dynasty, (A.D. 618–907) in which design was established through clear, simple shapes rather than a busy, decorative ornamentation. Many recent Disney films began their art development by looking back at the work of Walt Disney and his artists from the 1930s through the 1960s, and studying the techniques they applied, such as the styling for *Bambi*, in which the backgrounds provide a clear stage for the animation through lighting and design. Ric was pleased that they were actually able to incorporate those lessons into *Mulan*, while at the same time enabling *Mulan* to have its own unique look. "After all, I'm working for Disney because of the films by those guys who worked with Walt and what they accomplished," Ric explains.

Mulan abandoned by the army. Visual development art by Paul Felix.

Army on the march. Visual development art by Ric Sluiter.

Layout

The layout department, headed by Robert Walker, took the approved storyboard sequences and, following the needs of the story, the production design principles and the art direction set forth by Hans Bacher and Ric Sluiter, developed the workbook. The artists creating the workbook would determine if a scene was a long shot, a medium shot, or a close-up based on what was important for the scene to convey. If the audience was supposed to clearly understand a character's emotions, a close-up was used. A long shot was used when it was important to establish a character's relationship within the setting.

The strong influence the *Mulan* storyboard artists had on the final staging of the film can be seen in the thumbnail copies of storyboard drawings that are incorporated into the workbook along the top of the page.

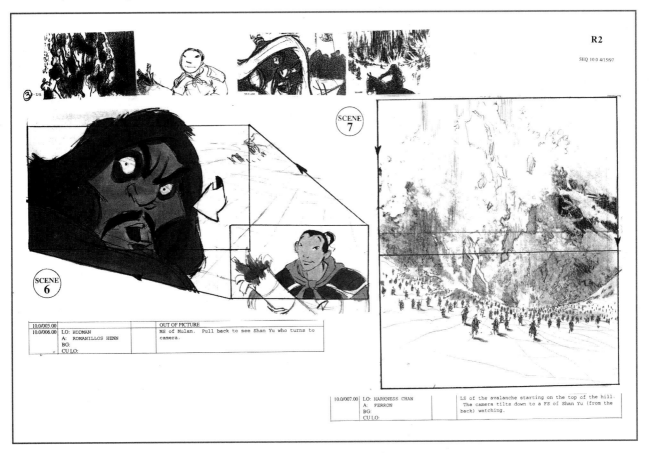

Workbook layouts by Robert Walker

49

The workbook artists also decided if it would be most effective and interesting if the viewer was looking straight into the scene, from up above, or from a low camera angle. Not only did the workbook show the characters who were in the scene and what their attitudes and actions were, but it also indicated what kind of camera movement may be involved—panning (side to side) or trucking (zooming in or out), for example. All these decisions were based on what the audience needs to know and what is the best way to present it. Eventually the workbook represented every sequence and scene in the film.

Workbook layout by Jeff Dickson

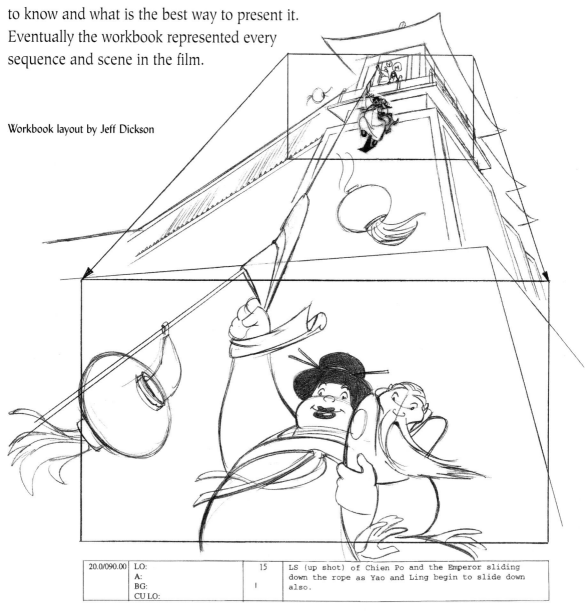

20.0/090.00	LO:	15	LS (up shot) of Chien Po and the Emperor sliding
	A:		down the rope as Yao and Ling begin to slide down
	BG:	I	also.
	CU LO:		

When designing the layout for a scene, the artist must follow the production design and art direction, as well as research those elements that will contribute an authentic look to architecture, furnishings, and the setting's landscape. The artist must also take into consideration where the character animation will be in the scene so that staging is clear for important actions.

Layout by Tom Humber

When the workbook layouts were approved by the directors, the full-size layout drawings were begun. A clean line drawing was produced, as well as a single color–tonal for every scene—some 1,650 scenes by the time the film was completed. Those layouts were then handed over to the artists who created the background paintings.

Tonals provide the background painters with an understanding of how the layout department envisions a scene will be painted. It shows how the characters will read against the background's light and dark areas.

Clean-up layout and tonal by Andy Harkness

Clean-up layout by Craig Grasso. Painting by Chuck Vollmer.

Background Paintings

Robert Stanton led the team of artists who painted the backgrounds for *Mulan*. Working closely with the layouts and the color keys produced under Ric Sluiter's guidance, the background paintings capture the story's visual sweep, provide an appropriate stage for its action, and reinforce the movie's emotional moods.

Many details observed during the trip to China found their way into the film's design and backgrounds. The drum tower that announces the arrival of the soldiers in Mulan's village was taken from an actual tower in a Chinese village. The moongate was an architectural detail the Disney travelers admired. They put one in Mulan's garden to provide a beautiful frame for her at one point during the song "Reflection." It also served to focus Mulan's attention on her parents during the evening when she makes her fateful decision.

Clean-up layout by Peter DeLuca. Painting by Xiangyuan Jie.

Clean-up layout by Peter DeLuca. Painting by Chuck Vollmer.

Character Animation

An animator has often been described as an actor with a pencil. The animator brings a character to life through a series of drawings that, when viewed in succession, create the illusion of movement. Depending upon how fast that movement will be, the number of actual drawings per character can be as much as twenty-four for every second of screen time.

"The magic of animation is when people totally believe in the emotions and reality of a character who has been brought to life through an artist's drawings and heart," Mark Henn says. However, movement alone is not enough to make a character believable. Character actions must be as varied as one sees in real life and be appropriate to the type of individual that character represents. Attitude of body and facial expression must also be clearly conveyed in order for that character to come alive. Additionally, the viewer must believe that the character has a soul and a mind. It is no wonder that in solving the challenges of bringing a character to life on the motion–picture screen, the animator finds himself believing in the reality of the drawings that emerge from the tip of his pencil.

Chien-Po demonstrates a joyous athleticism during a training exercise.

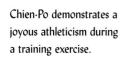

Rough animation of Chien-Po by Broose Johnson and clean-up animation by Tom Fish

54

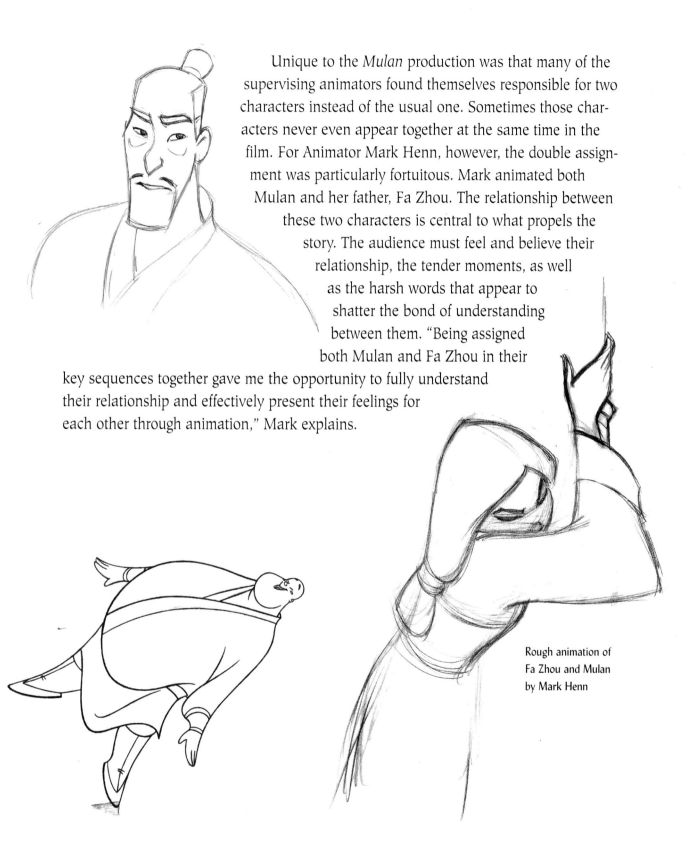

Unique to the *Mulan* production was that many of the supervising animators found themselves responsible for two characters instead of the usual one. Sometimes those characters never even appear together at the same time in the film. For Animator Mark Henn, however, the double assignment was particularly fortuitous. Mark animated both Mulan and her father, Fa Zhou. The relationship between these two characters is central to what propels the story. The audience must feel and believe their relationship, the tender moments, as well as the harsh words that appear to shatter the bond of understanding between them. "Being assigned both Mulan and Fa Zhou in their key sequences together gave me the opportunity to fully understand their relationship and effectively present their feelings for each other through animation," Mark explains.

Rough animation of
Fa Zhou and Mulan
by Mark Henn

MULAN

"Mulan is not just someone who accomplishes something in spite of the restrictions placed on her because she is a woman, but she is a person who achieves something extraordinary. Seeing her as an individual who was able to alter society's views and effect a positive change in those around her clarified the story for me. It was her strong personality traits that made the story happen; she's the catalyst," points out Barry Cook. And Mark Henn adds, "The trip to China gave me a chance to be in Mulan's home country and imagine how she would have lived and felt about her family and country. This was key to my understanding and development of her character."

Visual development art by Dean DeBlois

When character designs are explored, it is as much a search for personality through action as it is a character's physical features. Early on it was recognized that Mulan's independent spirit could be established through her relationship with her horse, Khan. Thus, many early drawings show those two characters together.

At one time during development, consideration was given to show Mulan as a youngster—a child interested in her father's military trappings. That aspect of her childhood was discarded so that when she leaves to take her father's place in the army, her decison is clearly the result of her love for her father, not some unrealized dream to be a soldier.

Visual development art by Carloine Hu

During training, Mulan is surprised by a too-helpful Mushu attaching the target to her arrow. Rough animation by Mark Henn.

"Can she do that?" a surprised Yao inquires when Mulan enthusiastically hugs the wise and understanding Emperor. Mark Henn provided the rough animation of Mulan, which was then matched with the animation drawing of the Emperor.

Mulan's clever, if unconventional, approach to problems, as well as her concern for her father, is established in her opening sequence. Production still.

SHANG

Shang is the young captain who unexpectedly has the burden of full leadership thrust upon him, along with the responsibility of unforseen decision-making.

Shang's supervising animator, Ruben Aquino, was born in Okinawa. He was drawn to working on *Mulan* because of his Asian heritage and the fact that Disney had never done an animated feature set in an Asian country.

"So much of Shang's personality was already there in the storyboards. I wanted to add to that and create a character who was believable as a strong, tough, commanding officer, but who also had a vulnerable side," Ruben said.

"So many little lessons emerge effortlessly from the characters. I'm fond of Shang because we see him learn that true leadership sometimes isn't about following rules," Pam Coats observes.

Character study by Ruben Aquino

Rough animation
by Ruben Aquino

"Shang is very stylized. His head shape is unique
for a Disney character in that it isn't the usual
circle or oval, but is angular, more like a
stretched-out stop sign," Ruben explained.

Newly appointed to the rank of captain,
Shang imagines for himself a career of
military achievement. Production still.

MUSHU

At one point in the story development, two dragons were proposed, each one's personality complementing the other's, as in the Yin and Yang symbol. This was abandoned for more effective storytelling through the role of a single character, and Mushu, the demoted Guardian dragon, found his place in the film.

Mushu was a challenging character to animate because even though he has arms and legs, they're attached to a snakelike body with a long neck. His anatomy doesn't relate to human proportions, but he still has to display recognizable human movements and gestures.

Visual development art by Chris Sanders

Visual development art of Yin and Yang by Caroline Hu

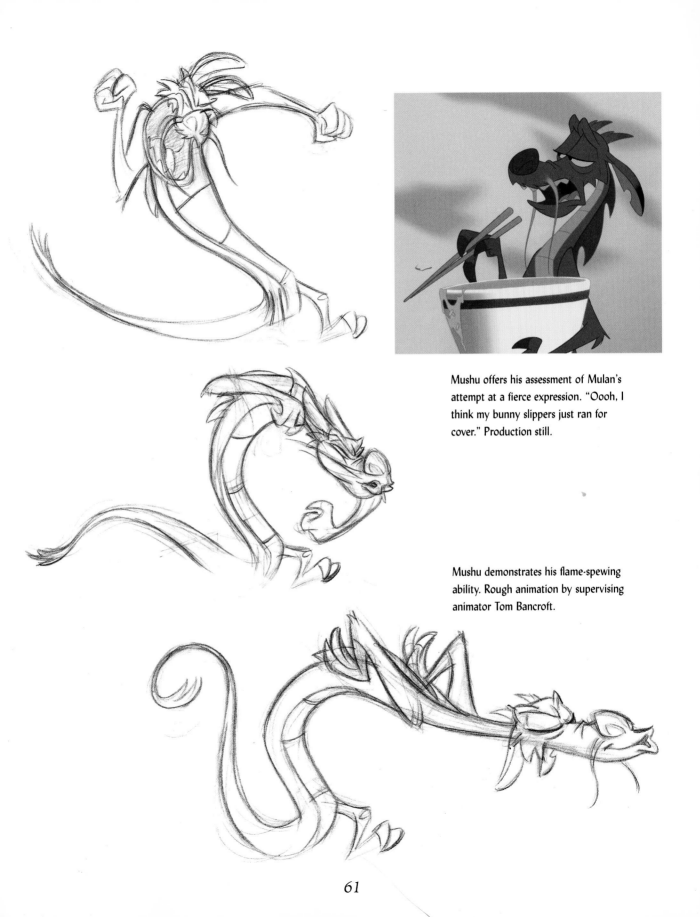

Mushu offers his assessment of Mulan's attempt at a fierce expression. "Oooh, I think my bunny slippers just ran for cover." Production still.

Mushu demonstrates his flame-spewing ability. Rough animation by supervising animator Tom Bancroft.

SHAN-YU

When Pres Romanillos saw the original development art for *Mulan*, he was impressed because it was so different. Having been one of the animators of Disney heroine Pocahontas, Pres eagerly accepted the chance to go in the opposite direction and be the supervising animator for Mulan's massive, feral villain, Shan-Yu.

As the actor behind the pencil, Pres had to get inside Shan-Yu and identify with this cunning, athletic predator. "Shan-Yu is not one of the Disney comic villains. He had to be a very real, believable threat to make the story work," Pres points out.

Character study by Pres Romanillos

Visual development art by Peter De Seve

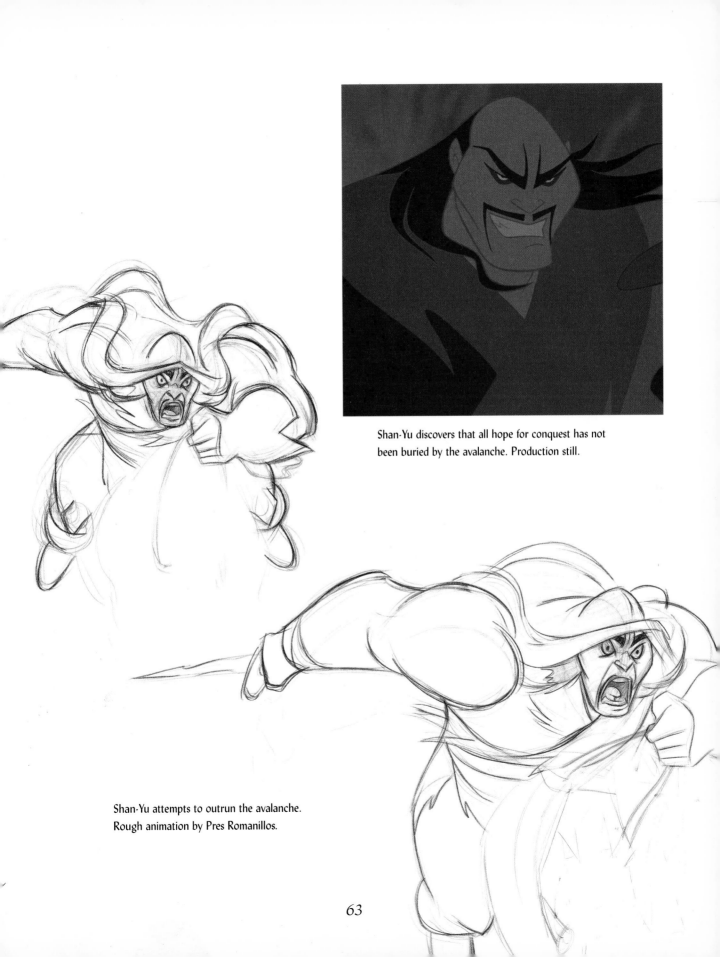

Shan-Yu discovers that all hope for conquest has not been buried by the avalanche. Production still.

Shan-Yu attempts to outrun the avalanche.
Rough animation by Pres Romanillos.

KHAN

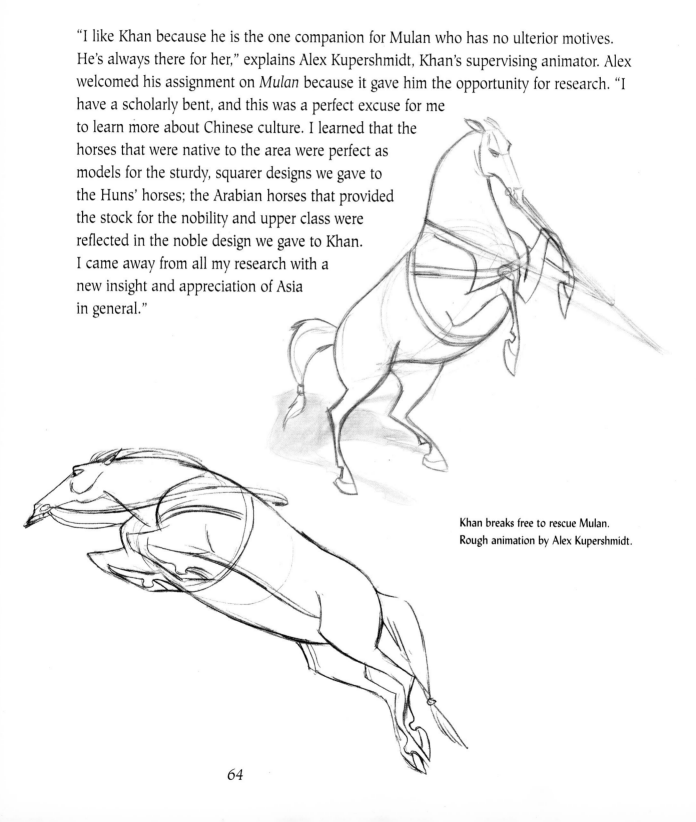

"I like Khan because he is the one companion for Mulan who has no ulterior motives. He's always there for her," explains Alex Kupershmidt, Khan's supervising animator. Alex welcomed his assignment on *Mulan* because it gave him the opportunity for research. "I have a scholarly bent, and this was a perfect excuse for me to learn more about Chinese culture. I learned that the horses that were native to the area were perfect as models for the sturdy, squarer designs we gave to the Huns' horses; the Arabian horses that provided the stock for the nobility and upper class were reflected in the noble design we gave to Khan. I came away from all my research with a new insight and appreciation of Asia in general."

Khan breaks free to rescue Mulan.
Rough animation by Alex Kupershmidt.

Alex explores Khan's various facial expressions and attitudes.

"I loved the color choice of black for Khan—it's so flattering. And it provided a perfect backdrop for other characters to act against. They 'read' well against that dark mass," Alex Kupershmidt points out. Production still.

CRI-KEE

For a while it looked as if Cri-Kee was the character almost no one wanted to see in *Mulan*. His presence was viewed as a hindrance, an unnecessary adjunct to the story's momentum; he was doomed to fall into cartoon limbo. But his early claims to Mushu about being lucky had a basis in reality. The cricket's own lucky charm came in the person of Roy Disney. Roy saw the potential in the little cricket, and encouraged the story artists to recognize the possibilities in his role. Cri-Kee became an effective character for Mushu to play off, a contrast to the little dragon's emotional temperament, as well as an additional source for comedy.

"Animating Cri-Kee required combining believable insectlike movements along with human emotions and motivations, so that he stood out as a distinct personality," says supervising animator Barry Temple. "Because Cri-Kee doesn't have a voice, he represents the purest form of animation. All his actions must clearly convey his thoughts and intentions."

Prelude to disaster: Cri-Kee takes advantage of a refreshing pause in the matchmaker's teacup. Production still.

CHI FU

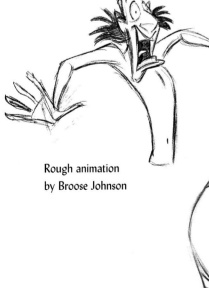

With a slightly devilish twinkle in his eye, Chi Fu's supervising animator Jeffrey Varab said that his character is one that people can often find in the classroom. He's not a true villain, but he's a definite antagonist, someone who has a desire to be liked by his teachers, but will step on his classmates. "I had to keep him subtle and low-key, but I did manage to instill in him certain irritating qualities I've known to exist in real life."

Rough animation by Jeffrey Varab

LING, YAO, AND CHIEN-PO

The rough attitudes of the recruits Mulan encounters at the army camp, their initial antagonism toward Mulan, and their subsequent rallying behind her and respect for her abilities were all brought clearly into focus by concentrating on Mulan's relationship with three main recruits, Ling, Yao, and Chien-Po.

Rough animation
by Broose Johnson

Rough animation
by Aaron Blaise

Rough animation by Broose Johnson

Effects Animation

Traditionally, the effects animator handles the movement of the things in an animated film that aren't characters. In *Mulan*, effects animation ranged from shadows, incense smoke, waves, and water splashes, to the thundering, theater-shaking avalanche that engulfs the invading Hun army. These effects are all created by hand in an exacting and painstaking process. In the case of the avalanche scenes, the effects crew took a full year to animate what would become less than a minute of screen time.

Lightning was designed to look like characters in Chinese writing. Animation by David Tidgwell. Production still.

Clouds and smoke both take their spiraling interior lines from designs in traditional Chinese art. Animation by Tony West. Production still.

... Head of Effects Dana Gregwin supervised ... ... the effects crew stylized natural elements, keeping them very two-dimesional and graphic, in order for them to fit harmoniously within the film's overall art styling. Smoke and water designs were based on how those elements were represented in ancient Chinese art, with the added requirement of devising how those designs, inspired by still illustrations, would then move in the medium of animation.

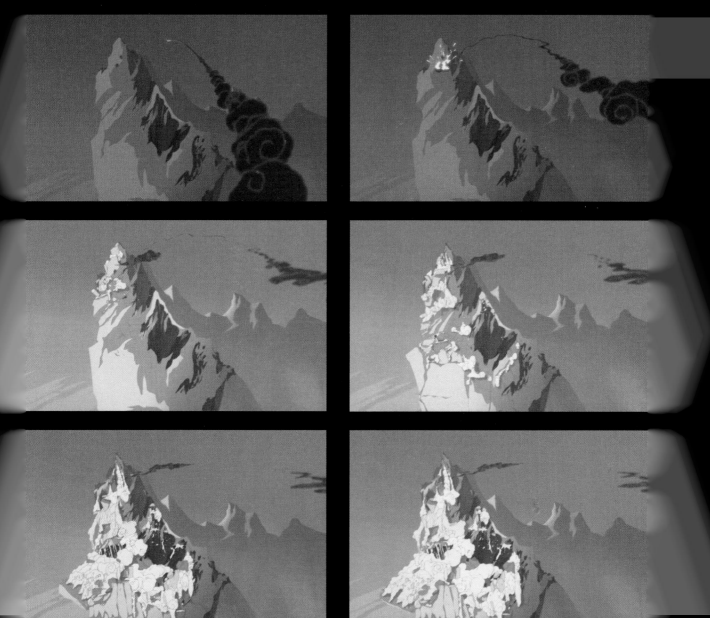

Mulan shoots a rocket into the mountain peak, causing the avalanche that will wipe out Shan-Yu's army. Animation of smoke,

Computer Animation

For more than ten years, Disney animated films have included some animation created by artists who use a computer instead of a pencil as their chosen tool. These artists are knowledgeable in both the use of a computer and in the timing and staging that are a part of effective animation. At first, computer-generated imagery, known as CGI, was seen as a way of handling the moving of objects, such as cars, in a more accurate and less time-consuming way than traditional hand-drawn means. Today the advancements in CGI, explains department head Eric Guaglione, "have made it an important component in adding value to a film and enhancing its cinematic quality, making it an integral part of a movie's storytelling."

During the trip to China, members of the development team were impressed by both the prevalence of flags, and the fact that there always seemed to be wind blowing.

The CGI unit added impressive, fluttering flags to scenes, capturing both a visual and an atmospheric aspect of the China trip.

The *Mulan* CGI unit was able to step in and work with the character animators so that, together, they could break new ground in the visuals used for animated storytelling. One of their collaborations is seen in the terrifying charge of the Huns through the Tung-Shao Pass.

Computer animation of flags by Darlene Hadrika.
Modeling by Mary Ann Pigora.

Computer animation of the Hun charge by Sandra Groeneveld and Tony Plett

Character animation provided the CGI animators with examples of how the Huns' horses would gallop across the snow, as seen in side and three-quarter views. The CGI artists then used those drawings as a guide, and developed and animated dimensional frames of the horses and their riders. They then applied the flat color tones that would fit the film's art direction, and outlined the characters in such a way that made them fit perfectly with the hand-drawn animation.

New Technology

Since *The Rescuers Down Under* (1990), the previous technique of handpainting the animators' drawings onto acetate cels was replaced by scanning the drawings into a computer, coloring them by computer, and incorporating them into the handpainted backgrounds, which, themselves, had also been transferred into the computer's digital file. This system, created by Disney technicians, is known as CAPS.

An artist creates a color model for Mulan on a CAPS monitor.

The fact that most of the production took place in Orlando, Florida, with a contributing staff who remained at the home facility for Feature Animation in Burbank, California, added a logistic problem that was solved by new technology. Every day various members of the Florida creative teams linked up for face-to-face meetings with their California colleagues via CLI hookups. More than just large screen television linkups, these meetings enabled immediate show-and-tell review of artwork, as well as discussions for proposed new directions for the unreeling of the film's story. Art created on one coast could be instantaneously viewed in close-up detail on another. Without this new, efficient technology, this type of bicoastal collaboration would have been unwieldy, if not impossible.

It's a Wrap

Millions of man hours. Miles of paper. Thousands of pencils worn down to nubs. Technological breakthroughs. Hundreds of catered meals for those work sessions that pushed their way into the late hours of the evening and the weekends. The making of *Mulan* consumed the time, energy, emotions, and inspiration of its contributors.

What emerged is a film that stands out visually from the classic Disney animated features that precede it. *Mulan* is a movie with a soul that sings the praises of an individual who defies tradition out of an unselfish devotion to family, who uses the strengths of her spirit and mind to achieve the seemingly impossible, and whose unique courage earns her the respect of her contemporaries and the love of succeeding generations.

And *Mulan* is a film that has earned the passionate devotion of those who helped bring it into being.

Fa Zhou: The greatest gift and honor is having you for a daughter.

"From the beginning, I wanted to work on something I could be truly proud of, and *Mulan* has been exactly that!"

–Hans Bacher